"Gonzalez amazes in his ability to create life on the page—this is not a story, it's Ybor City, its sights, smells sounds and its people who make it mad, hopeless, crazy and ultimately beautiful, recounted in painterly detail by the sensitive young boy who saw it all up close."

—Trebor Healey, author of the award-winning
Through It Came Bright Colors,
and *A Horse Named Sorrow*

"The authenticity and honesty of Gonzalez' stories rings true in a time of great freedom, but rough politics. Several of the dramatic tales are told through the eyes of an impressionable young person. Told simply, with warmth and humanity, these tender but unsentimental stories will get under your skin"!

—Connie Kronlokken, novelist.

"Against the background of a working-class community in a 1940s factory town, Gonzalez brings to life the vibrant color of this time and place, with stories of love, politics and gallantry, told by a young boy coming of age with his personal sexual identity."

—Guy Biederman, writer, publisher

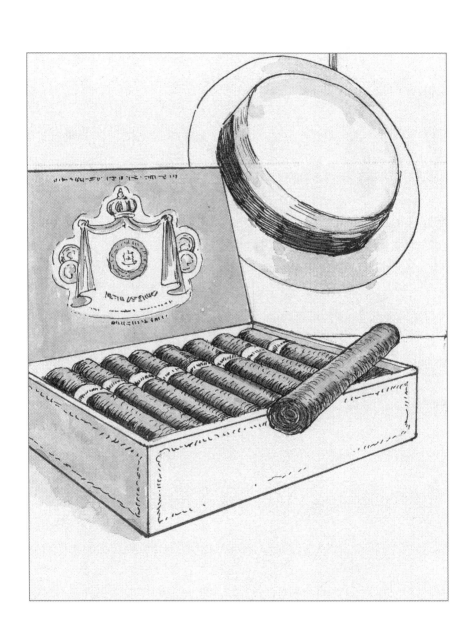

S CIGAR CITY Stories

Tales of Old Ybor City

Emilio Gonzalez-Llanes

Illustrations: Susan St. Thomas, Occidental, Ca

iUniverse, Inc.
Bloomington

Cigar City Stories
Tales of Old Ybor City

iUniverse books may be ordered through booksellers or by contacting:

iUniverse
1663 Liberty Drive
Bloomington, IN 47403
www.iuniverse.com
1-800-Authors (1-800-288-4677)

Because of the dynamic nature of the Internet, any web addresses or links contained in this book may have changed since publication and may no longer be valid. The views expressed in this work are solely those of the author and do not necessarily reflect the views of the publisher, and the publisher hereby disclaims any responsibility for them.

Any people depicted in stock imagery provided by Thinkstock are models, and such images are being used for illustrative purposes only.
Certain stock imagery © Thinkstock.

ISBN: 978-1-4759-5093-9 (sc)
ISBN: 978-1-4759-5095-3 (hc)
ISBN: 978-1-4759-5094-6 (ebk)

Library of Congress Control Number: 2012917885

Printed in the United States of America

iUniverse rev. date: 09/25/2012

CONTENTS

ACKNOWLEDGEMENTS

I'm grateful to my sisters, Alice Gonzalez and Sylvia Espinola, for sharing their memories and stories of growing up in Ybor City. I especially want to thank Amie Hill, whose keen eyes edited and polished the final manuscript, and all of you helped make this book a reality: Guy Biederman, Jorge Rodriguez, Rebecca Fernandez, Connie Kronlokken, Jim Metzger, Aron Asbell, Susan St. Thomas, Marylu Downing, and many others who read these stories and provided valuable feedback and encouragement.

INTRODUCTION

In 1885, Vincent Martinez Ybor, a Spanish entrepreneur, purchased forty acres of mudflats east of Tampa and built a "company town" of tall red-brick factories and small wood-frame houses for the workers. Over the next forty years, this community of immigrant cigar-makers from Cuba, Spain and Italy grew into a thriving industry that made Tampa the "Cigar Capital of the World."

Guided by customs from their homeland and socialist ideals popular at the time, the workers built social clubs and established benevolent societies that provided cradle-to-grave medical care for twenty-five cents per week. The cigar-makers also organized strong labor unions. Strikes, lockouts, boycotts, and violence followed. Kidnappings of labor leaders, lynchings, and false arrests of the "communist" agitators were carried out by the Anglo authorities.

The Great Depression of the Thirties struck a major blow to the vibrant cigar industry; the public could not afford cigars and switched to cigarettes. By 1940, cigar-making machines were introduced into the factories, one machine replacing thirty workers. In 1959, ninety percent of all cigars made in Tampa were machine-made. The urban renewal of the 1960s struck a deathblow to Ybor City; thousands of cigar-makers' homes and businesses were leveled by bulldozers, and an interstate highway stormed through the dying neighborhood.

I was born and raised in Ybor City and graduated from Jefferson High School. My parents and most of my relatives worked in the cigar factories. Some of the stories in this book are reflections on growing up and coming of age in this colorful community that no longer exists. Other stories are based on true historical incidents. I hope you enjoy reading this book as much as I did writing it.

—Emilio Gonzalez-Llanes, Santa Rosa, California, 2012

EL PARAISO

José hung the white canvas apron around my neck. "It's time you wore this, Rafa; last summer you were too young, but this year you can help me collect the money and keep an eye on the women customers—they're a bunch of thieves."

I slid my hands into the deep pockets of the new apron. "Thank you, José. Can I take it home?"

"Just to wash it, otherwise leave it here."

I reached behind me and tied the straps. "Can I get more pay, too?"

"More pay?" José howled. "I'm two months behind on the mortgage, my children need shoes, and you want more pay?" He walked down the narrow aisle of the store to the cash register.

"O.K. I'll pay you thirty cents an hour instead of twenty-five. Now, get to work! Clean up this place, it looks like a toilet, not a food store."

As he spoke, José Sanchez, his straight hair slicked back with Brilliantine, wrinkled the large nose that was the centerpiece of his Cuban face. He'd left Cuba when he was eighteen; a fight in a cane field—dueling with machetes over a woman, he claimed—had left him with a big scar on his jaw and without work. The cigar company paid his passage to Tampa, and he got a job as a shipping clerk at El Paraiso the busiest cigar factory in Ybor City, Perfecto Garcia & Company, nicknamed *El Paraiso* by early immigrants from Cuba because of the flowering magnolia and paradise trees that surrounded the four-story brick building. In five years, José had saved enough to start a small business selling fruits and vegetables, located just across the street from the factory.

José's Fruiteria was a combination fruit-stand, grocery store and commissary. It was housed in a former garage with a back door that opened into a large shaded yard where every day a dozen Sicilian women, all cigar-makers, ate their lunches of salami, cucumber and tomato-sauce sandwiches.

Lola Valdez-Riley, a neighbor and regular customer, always shopped near closing time on her way home. I watched her pinch the avocados, smell the cantaloupes and toss a seedless grape into her mouth.

"*Quanto le debo, M'ijo?*" Lola didn't just say this; she sang it, one hand on her hip and her foot tapping the floor with the open toe of her high-heeled shoes.

"Two ears of corn, three onions, two sweet potatoes, a dozen eggs, a Spanish *chorizo*, and a small bottle of sweet vermouth. That comes to two dollars and ten cents, Senorita." I avoided her probing eyes.

"Listen *hermoso*, please don't call me Senorita." She leaned closer. "I am not a virgin, I am not a wife, but a lonely widow. Call me Senora." She adjusted a bra strap and reached for her purse. Her long auburn hair tumbled down her face and stuck to her glossy red lips.

"Rafa, Lola doesn't have to pay." José announced from the front door, "Give her the money back."

"What?" I was puzzled. José had told me no discounts for anyone.

"This lovely young lady is a pillar of our community and has a good position at the factory. We need to be good to her."

I dug into my apron pocket and returned Lola's cash.

"You'll make a good cashier, *machito*." She stroked my curly brown hair. "I handle thousands of dollars every week at the factory, but none of it is mine,"

"Let me walk you home, *querida*." José picked up her grocery bag, offered his arm to Lola, and the two of them strolled down the street, whispering secrets under her red parasol.

Ten years earlier, Lola had spent two weeks in jail for defying a ban on picketing for higher wages in front of El Paraiso. In the settlement, the Union demanded that she be given a clerk's job in the office. On paydays, she stuffed tiny envelopes with cash and coins to pay the workers.

Her full figure, curves front and back, made her a constant target for Latin men's eyes. On her three-block walk to the factory in the early morning, cigar-smoking men, flush from their cognac and *café solo,* whistled and hooted, shouted proposals of marriage, expounded poetic fantasies, or just plain grunted at the sight of this lovely creature. She lived alone, but lately she'd been escorted to the Sunday-matinee tea-dances at the Centro Español Club by Santiago Nuñez, a recent arrival from Cuba who had become the new doorman at El Paraiso. He was younger than Lola, tall, with broad shoulders and muscled arms like a blacksmith.

"Is Lola your girlfriend?" I asked José. We sat at the picnic table in the backyard after closing up the store.

"That's none of your business." José took a slug from a silver flask he carried in his back pocket. "I'm a married man with three children."

I snacked on a Cuban sandwich. José did not eat. He looked tired.

"Lots of husbands in Ybor City have girlfriends." I continued.

"Not me Rafa. Lola's husband, Patrick, was my friend. You heard about the murder didn't you?"

"Murder? What murder?"

"They called it a suicide, so Lola got no insurance, no pension."

José chomped on his cheroot and spit on the ground.

"Lola's husband, a police sergeant, asked too many questions about *bolita,* the Cuban lottery run by the Mafia. They found him in his squad car on Palmetto Beach with a twelve-gauge shotgun between his legs, his head blown away."

It was still dark on Saturday morning when José and I got back from the farmers' market in his '46 Chevy panel truck packed with bushels of fruit and vegetables. With sisal rope, we hung bananas and *platanos* to the beams that held up the tattered tarp over the sidewalk. José's legs shook as he lifted the heavy stems. Across the street, waiters in white jackets carried large pots of Cuban coffee and steamed milk to pour *café con leche* for the cigar-rollers arriving at their workbench. Saturday was payday at El Paraiso.

The armored truck that brought the payroll pulled up in front of the factory at precisely 8:00 a.m. as it did every week. But that day something was different; the driver was alone, and no guard accompanied him. He lugged big bags filled with bills and coins up the wide wooden steps of the factory to the office. making two trips. When the armored truck pulled away from the curb the driver waved and smiled at José. José did not wave back.

Streaks of lightning flashed nearby. Within minutes, large raindrops turned to steam on the hot red-brick streets lined with granite curbstones. People scattered for shelter in doorways, under awnings; wind-driven clouds released slanted sheets of water on a thousand tin roofs, creating a roar that sounded like a speeding freight train. Then just as suddenly as it arrived, the thunderstorm moved on, the sun came out, and people emerged from the shadows.

"I'll be back in an hour, Rafa," José said. "I have to go to the bank. Be sure to collect the tabs owed by these women."

"Don't worry José, I can handle it."

José was sweating more than usual and chain-smoking Chesterfields instead of his usual cigar.

"If I'm not back by closing time, lock up and take the money home." He gunned the panel truck and scratched off down the narrow alley.

I shelved canned goods and mopped up pools of water that had leaked through the roof during the storm. In the backyard, a hairless dog snored in the shade of a banyan tree, amid branches that had spread like an octopus and touched the ground to root there.

When José got back to the store, the streets were lined with people gawking at the ambulances, police cars and vans jammed in front of El Paraiso. The news about the hold-up at the factory spread like brushfire in Ybor City. The workers would not be paid until Monday. Depending on who you talked to, the burglars had taken between fifty and one hundred thousand dollars.

The hold-up at El Paraiso made front-page news in all the papers; even the *Miami Herald* ran the story. *La Gaceta*, Ybor City's Spanish,/English/Italian daily ran a special bulletin:

BOLD HOLDUP AT PERFECTO GARCIA

TAMPA—Just before noon on Saturday, two armed men wearing stocking masks broke into the offices of Perfecto Garcia cigar factory in Ybor city and stole the week's payroll, valued at more than $50,000. The doorman, Santiago Nuñez, said he heard a man's voice saying, "Abre la puerta, Santiago." He opened the door and the thieves swiftly chloroformed him and tied him up with sisal rope. Lola Valdez-Riley, the payroll clerk, was also gassed, gagged and tied to her chair. Senorita Valdez said that when she came to, her grandmother's diamond wedding *ring was missing from her finger. The two robbers emptied the safe and drove away in a stolen 1938 Chevy sedan.*

"What time did you get to work today?" the police detective asked José.

"Same as always, 6:00 o'clock." José looked directly into the policeman's eyes.

"And have you been here all day?"

"Sure; who else is going to run this business?"

"Did you notice anything unusual across the street at El Paraiso?"

"No, pretty much the same crap week after week."

"How about you, son?" the detective asked me, "Did you notice anything different at the factory this morning?"

A stern glance from José was all I needed to shut my mouth.

I lowered my eyes and choked out a whisper: "No sir, not a thing"

For the next two days, Ybor City's economy stood still. No one had money to pay debts, buy food, or eat at the local restaurant. Saturday's lottery tickets were sold on credit. The phrase *"Abre la puerta, Santiago"* was adopted by the Cuban workers and became a popular *chiste,* or joke, to be used on almost any occasion.

The factory owners sacked Santiago for incompetence, but he immediately got hired as a guard for the armored-car company. The trauma of the holdup was too much for Lola, who resigned for health reasons and never came back to El Paraiso.

As expected, rumors about the holdup spread throughout Ybor City, and the possibilities of an "inside job" with payoffs, and bribes became the hot topic of nightly discussions at the Centro Español and the Cuban Club. But eventually, when all the conspiracy theories had been aired and other subjects began to dominate the news, memories of the holdup faded.

"Rafa, I'm sorry, but after this week, I won't need you anymore." José digs into the cash register for my weekly salary.

"But it's still summer! School doesn't start for a month!"

"I know, son, but I've sold the business to a Sicilian family and they won't be needing you." He hands me my pay.

"Sold the business? What are you going to do now, José?"

"I'm moving back to Cuba. I've booked passage for me and my family on the *SS Florida,* sailing from Miami to Havana on Sunday."

"I'll miss you, José; I've learned a lot from you."

"You'll do all right, Rafa. You can be trusted, and that's important." He walks to the back door. "Come, I have a present for you. It's under the banyan tree."

A late-model used Schwinn Phantom bicycle waited for me in the backyard.

"Wow, it's beautiful, José! Thank you! Thank you! Has Lola seen it?"

"No. Haven't you heard?"

"Heard what?"

José strikes a wooden match on the leather sole of his shoe and re-lights his *Habana Puro*.

"Lola and Santiago eloped to Georgia and got married. They're living in West Tampa now, and she's opened a store to buy and sell gold jewelry."

My mouth falls open, but I say nothing. In the back yard, colonies of monarch butterflies blanket the solitary Paradise tree and savor its bitter berries.

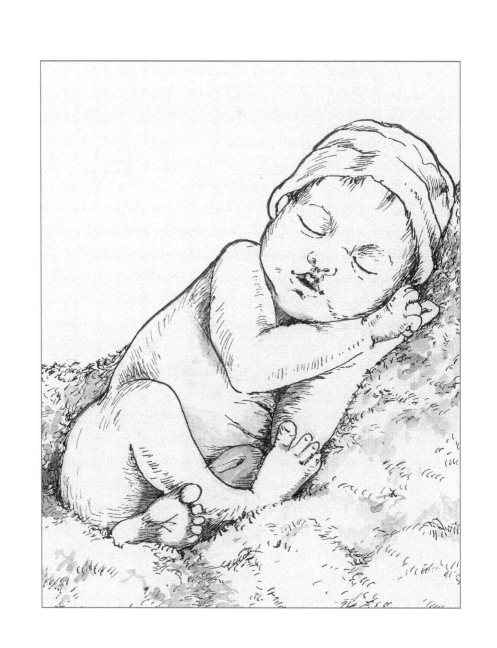

NEW BABY

I'm sitting on the edge of my parents' double bed reading my birth certificate, newly found in a shoebox under the bed, buried among old photos, clippings, and faded Christmas cards. It certifies that I was "born alive" in Hillsborough County, Tampa, Florida, at 1:27 p.m. on November 21, 1937. In the blank labeled "color or race," someone had scribbled the word "white".

It also tells me that my father, Francisco Gonzalez, 39, a cigar-maker for 23 years, was born in Cuba and that my mother, Margarita Llanes, 37, born in Tampa, does "housework" at home. This is a yellowed photostat of the original certificate on file with the State in Tallahassee. The fuzzy signature at the bottom reads "Josefina Valenti, Midwife." She had also delivered my sister Carmen two years earlier on this same bed.

Josefina, a former nun, immigrated to Ybor City in the 1920s, together with many families from, the Magazzolo Valley in Sicily. Most of them got work in the cigar factories, but using skills she learned as a nurse, Josefina built a thriving business delivering babies, for an affordable fee that included pre- and post-natal care.

She lives close by, and I often see her in a white nurse's uniform and cap marching to the home of some lucky couple. She carries a black leather satchel, like a doctor's, on all her calls. After her visit, a baby usually appears in the household. I used to think she brought the babies in that mysterious black bag.

On hot summer evenings after dinner, our family sits on the long porch that stretches across the front of our faded yellow house that had been a moonshine distillery during prohibition. Avocados and papayas grow in the backyard, a huge mango tree shades the bedrooms from the intense heat, and brick pilings lift the house above the hot sands. We greet neighbors strolling past, and everyone is talking about the end of the War, or Roosevelt's passing. Carmen and I spend the evening playing games of imagination and make-believe.

"Who's your favorite hero, Jorge?" She asks, shooing mosquitoes from her bare legs.

"I want to be like Robin, live in a cave with Batman and share a life of crime-fighting."

"Not me," says Carmen. "I want to be strong, like Wonder Woman and beat up all the guys."

Father puffs away on his cigar and leans back in his wicker rocking chair. Mother crochets in silence. Most nights she tells us stories that she makes up as she goes along. But tonight, she has a distant look in her eyes.

She turns to face my father, "Paco, we have to talk." She puts down her needle and thread. "Carmen and Jorge, go inside; it's almost bedtime."

"No. Let them stay, q*uerida*. I want no secrets in this house."

"You may not want to hear this, but I'm six months pregnant. The baby is due in July."

"Impossible," he says. "You can't be pregnant at your age, and we don't need another mouth to feed."

"It's true, *mi amor*," she wipes her eyes. "I've been to see Josefina. She thinks it will be another boy."

He snuffs his cigar and places it on the handrail. "I'm going to bed now. Tomorrow we can talk about resolving this situation. *Buenas noches*, Rita."

Carmen is overjoyed by the news. I hate it. I will no longer be *"el bebito"* in our family and we'll have this screaming little boy to look after. I walk to the far end of the porch and hang over the railing. Carmen presses her ear to my mother's stomach to see if she can hear the baby sloshing around.

My father learned the art of cigar-making in Cuba. By the age of twenty-two, he was working as a finisher, the person who gives each cigar its final form and wrapper. In Ybor City, he's one of the top finishers at Perfecto Garcia. At the end of the workday, Father stashes a few unfinished cigars into his shirt to take home, smoke, and give to his friends. On paydays he sells the *Communist Daily Worker* on the factory steps. Most evenings after dinner he joins his male coworkers at the Cuban Club to play dominos and talk politics.

"Look, *querida*, you must understand," Father reaches for the sugar bowl on the kitchen table. "Since the War ended, more machines are being installed. Last week thirty workers on my floor were laid off and replaced by cigar-making machines and low-paid women to operate them."

"Why are you telling me this?" Mother asks.

"Because I could lose my job any day, and, I can't get work in America. I don't speak their language."

Wonder Woman and Robin crawl under the house and lie with their backs in the sand underneath the kitchen floor.

"It would not be fair to bring a child into this uncertain situation," he pauses. "I don't want you to have this baby. My sister in Havana can take you to a doctor who will fix this. It's safe and legal."

"Fix me?" She laughs. "But I'm not broken. I'm just doing what women do naturally—have babies." She walks to the refrigerator.

"I don't know why I got pregnant so close to menopause, but this unformed soul inside my body is taking a chance with me and deserves to see the light of day. Please thank your sister." Her footsteps echo down the long hallway and out the front door.

My mother is not someone to fool with. She's an activist and feminist who marched in picket lines during the labor strife of the thirties and led a boycott to protest poor working conditions. In a portrait photo taken by Uncle Oscar when she was eighteen, she looks like a movie star. She poses with a serene look, her dark hair pulled back from her face, her deep brown eyes and elegant Roman nose crowned by thick eyebrows that meet in the middle. Her lips are pomegranate red, even with no lipstick. Now in her late forties, she's gained weight, her hairy chin sags a bit, and her nose is larger, but I still think she's beautiful.

"What's menopause?" I ask Carmen. We're at the kitchen table doing our schoolwork.

"I'm not sure, Jorge." She looks up from her math problems. "But I think it's some kind of infection. I know it only happens to older women."

I go back to scrolling cursive letters onto long lined paper. No more block letters like we learned in early grades. The teacher says this will help us to develop our own signature, something that will distinguish us for the rest of our lives.

"Did you pick up the diapers and baby bottles?" Carmen asks.

"I sure did. The clerk at La Economica put them on our tab."

"Remember, our baby brother will be arriving any day now. Josefina said we must have plenty of clean towels and pans of hot water ready to go."

Carmen taught me English when I started school, and later she showed me how to dance the mambos and jitterbugs of the day. When bullies followed me home from school, she defended me. She was smarter and stronger than most of the boys, climbed trees, went fishing, and played on the school's softball team.

These days Mother spends a lot of time in bed. She naps lying on her side, her abdomen swollen as big as a watermelon. In the evening she falls asleep in the rocking chair. Carmen and I have taken over the household chores, her sister, Tia Maria, is cooking meals and our cousin Isabel takes care of us after school.

When father first arrived from Cuba, Tia Maria was his first choice for a bride. But she turned him down flat. "You drink too much, you gamble and womanize, and you've been married before," she told him. So he proposed to Margarita, the younger sister, and she accepted. Her brothers stayed away from the wedding, and bad feelings still linger today.

"Rita may not be the greatest cook, but at least she can fry an egg," Father says, and pushes away the breakfast plate Tia Maria has fixed for him.

"Be grateful and eat what the Lord provides." She stirs a pot of beans on the stove. "You men are all the same; nothing is ever good enough for you."

"Ever meet a man who's good enough for you, Maria Teresa?"

"No man has ever touched me. I'm intact, and I'll be buried this way." She slams the cleaver into cutting board.

A piercing scream comes from the bedroom.

"It's time. It's time," Mother yells. "*Vengan pronto*! Get Joséfina, *por favor*."

Tia rushes into the bedroom. Father puts on his hat and says, "Carmen, stay here. Help your aunt. Boy, you come with me. We'll be right back, Maria Teresa."

We dash to Josefina's house in father's '37 Chevy. He chatters all the way. "This entire situation could have been avoided." He sounds angry.

"Each birth costs me five dollars. I pay Josefina on time, twenty-five cents a week. Sometimes I can't pay, but I make it up in other ways. She's a very nice lady."

In fifteen minutes, we're back with Josefina in tow. She immediately takes charge and starts giving orders. "Maria, fill an ice-bag. Bring all the towels you can find and a pail of hot water. The rest of you stay in the living room and out of the way."

An hour goes by. Father paces the hallway, checks his pocket watch. Carmen and I play cat's cradle on the sofa. A mockingbird roosts in our mango tree and sings a medley of his favorite tunes. The cool shadow of a passing cloud cuts through the blanket of midsummer heat hanging over Ybor City.

"Paco! Paco, come quick! Something is wrong!" Josefina yells from the bedroom. Father dashes into the bedroom, leaves the door open.

"*Que pasa? Que pasa?*" he asks. I've never seen him so nervous.

"*Lo siento*, Francisco, but the baby is breeched. We must get Margarita to the hospital right away."

"The hospital? Why?" Tia asks. "In Cuba midwives birth breeched babies all the time. I've seen women in the cane fields, get down on all fours and have their baby without drugs or doctors. You can do it, Josefina."

"I'm sorry, I can't take a chance. I could lose my license."

Papi cradles mother in his arms, carries her down the steep front steps and lays her on the narrow back seat of his car. She looks up and smiles at us as they speed off to Centro Austuriano Hospital.

Carmen and I go to bed at midnight, still no word from the hospital. I can't fall asleep. I have a feeling something awful is going to happen.

Early the next morning, I hear Papi's car pull up in front of the house. He doesn't get out right away. He sits behind the wheel and stares into the foggy sunrise on Twentieth Avenue. Then he sits on the edge of his rocking chair, elbows on his knees and face in his hands. I've never seen him cry before. I cry, too. Carmen holds me.

"Come here, children. I have something to tell you." His eyes are swollen and red. He's not smoking.

He embraces us. "Your mother won't be coming home. They couldn't stop the bleeding. She passed away at three this morning." He sobs openly.

He blows his nose. "But God has sent us a beautiful baby girl to take her place—eight pounds, with a full head of black hair, and she looks just like Margarita."

I cry on my pillow for the rest of the morning. Carmen gets into one of her silent moods and sits high on a limb in the avocado tree. Tia Maria never cries. She puts new sheets on the crib and fixes lunch for us. But I can't eat, and neither can Carmen. In the afternoon, A.P. Boza, the funeral director, has father sign a few papers, then hangs a black wreath on our front door and drives away.

"Let me see the baby," Carmen says. "I want to see what she looks like."

"All babies look the same, red, wrinkled and wet," Josefina's holding the bundled infant in her arms. She parts the blanket and raises the baby's head.

"Wow. She's beautiful," Carmen exclaims. "Can I hold her?"

"Later, you can. I just fed her and it's time for her nap. How about you, Jorge? Want to take a look?"

"Not now," I say, averting my eyes, "I've seen babies before. Besides, I have to set up the folding chairs for the wake." I make myself very busy.

Food starts arriving around four: baked chicken, black beans, yellow rice, fried plantains, boiled shrimp, smoked mullet and *bollitos de pan*, followed by several salads and desserts of *flan* and *arroz con leche.* The men sit on wooden folding chairs on the porch, smoke cigars and exchange stories about life in Cuba.

Their cigar-lighting is like a ritual: each smoker bites into the cigar and tears a small piece from the rounded head, and then rolls it in his mouth to wet it with saliva and re-forms it. A wooden match, scratched into flame, is held to the other end and twirled as the smoker puffs, exhaling bluish-gray clouds and finishing with a sigh of satisfaction as the cigar tip glows on its own.

The women sit in a circle around the open coffin in the parlor. Maria Zorilla, my mother's best friend, never stops crying. She goes into convulsions with each new face that shows up.

"He could have been more careful," I hear Tia whisper to one of the ladies. "But men must satisfy their urges."

I stand by the window and wonder what Robin would do if he were in my skin.

"Jorge and Carmen, it's bedtime," Tia intones. "Pay your respects to your mother one last time. We'll leave for the cemetery early in the morning. She'll be buried at Woodlawn next to our mother."

Carmen and I stand hand-in-hand before the cheap wooden box holding a cold body made to look like my mother when she was much younger. She's dressed in a fancy embroidered silk dress I've never seen her wear, and the grin on her face is not hers.

The morning after the burial I wake up in a cold sweat. I dash to the kitchen to see if Mother is there making our *café con leche* and *pan con mantequilla*—buttered toast. But the kitchen is quiet, empty. Later, Father drives Carmen and me to school, the same as always, as if nothing's happened. Tia Maria stays to take care of infant Anna.

At school all day I keep hoping that it's a mistake that maybe the hospital switched patients and Mother will be home when we get there. But instead we find Father and Tia Maria huddled at the kitchen table conversing in hushed tones. Carmen and I stand on the back porch on either side of the screen door and listen.

"I cannot thank you enough, Maria Teresa, for all your help during this difficult period." He touches her hand. She pulls away.

"I'm not doing it for you, Paco. I'm doing it for my dear sister, Rita. She was the only person in the world I loved and trusted." She walks to the stove, turns on the burner under the coffee pot. "What's going to happen to the children?"

"I'm not sure, Maria." He lights his cigar, something my mother did not allow in the house. "My sister Eva said they can go and live with her in West Tampa."

"Forgive me, Paco, but I think your sister has her hands full taking care of her sick husband. I have lots of room at my house; they can come and live with me at the family home. The two older ones can take care of Baby Anna."

He stands next to Maria and takes her hand in his.

"Listen, Maria, I know that you and I don't always get along, but I think the simplest thing would be for you to move in with us. You can have the front bedroom, sleep in Rita's bed, and you won't have to take a job; I will provide for you and the children."

A rooster crows in the neighbor's yard. Carmen squeezes closer to the screen door.

"We have to finish what we started," he says.

"What we started was finished a long time ago, Francisco Gonzalez!" She retreats to the table. "Have you no shame? Your wife's body is still warm in the grave and you're proposing to her sister? Are you mad?"

"You broke my heart a long time ago when you said no, Maria, and now you want to break my heart again by taking my children away."

"They will still be your responsibility, Mr. Gonzalez. I expect you to come and see them at least once a week, keep us supplied with coffee, milk and bread, pay their health insurance, and show them some love."

That same day, the crib and baby furniture are moved to Tia Maria's. Carmen and I pack all our belongings, including the shoebox of old photos with my birth certificate, into moving boxes,. My cousin Danny and his friends load our beds, dressers, and clothes into a hired wagon and deliver them to the family home on Sixteenth Street. By the end of the month, my father sells the remaining furniture in the yellow house as well as the double bed that he shared with my mother, and rents a room at Josefina's.

At Tia Maria's house, my main duty is taking care of baby Anna; she seems to look different every day. Her oriental eyes, inherited from a distant and never-mentioned Chinese ancestor, are wide open now, and she smiles a lot. After dinner every night, I diaper and dress her, feed her a bottle of milk laced with Cuban coffee, and rock her gently to sleep.

PAPER DOLL

I steer my second-hand Schwinn over iron streetcar tracks on Michigan Avenue in Ybor City, enjoying the sensation of its balloon tires coasting smoothly over the ruts. I pedal up and down the red-brick streets and sling rolled-up copies of the *Tampa Daily Times* onto porches. Some hit the window-screen or land in the yard. Once I knocked over Dona Gabriela's African violets; that cost me a two weeks' subscription.

My route takes me past rows of shotgun houses and small bungalows built by the factory owners to house immigrant cigar-makers from Cuba, Spain, and Italy. Tropical fruit trees—avocados, mangos, *platano*s, and key limes—grow in the sandy backyards. Housewives in printed housedresses sweep sidewalks, and husbands in straw boaters sit on tiny front porches and smoke cigars.

I get done with my deliveries by four PM, except on Saturdays when I collect twenty-five cents from each customer. I give my earnings to my mother for household expenses. Today, I finish early and stop at La Brisa Café on Fifteenth Street for a Dr. Pepper and a Milky Way.

"Hey punk, I'm gonna smash your face in," It's Jesse Jordan. He sneaks up from behind, grabs my collar and pushes my head against the door of the Café. He jams his knee into my stomach. "Why'd you push me in the hall yesterday, Paper Doll?" He gave me that nickname one time when he saw me cutting out paper dolls with my sisters.

"I didn't push you. I didn't even see you yesterday." I resolve not to cry this time.

"Yes you did! Don't lie to me, asshole." He knees me again. "Next time I see you, I'm going to beat the hell out of you." He shoves me to the ground and runs off laughing with his buddies.

"Why didn't you push him back?" It's my sister Anna, who's seen the whole thing from the sidewalk.

"What? Are you crazy? He's much bigger than me. I wouldn't have a chance." I stuff my torn shirt into my jeans.

"Sooner or later, you're going to have to stand up to him, or he'll never leave you alone."

I'm tall and skinny, wear thick glasses and get pushed around a lot by the other boys, who know I won't fight back. What I fear most is running into Jesse Jordan, a bully who's been held back in school for a year because of bad grades and poor attendance. Older than the rest of us seventh-graders, he catches bullfrogs at the lake, sticks firecrackers in their mouths and blows them up, one by one. His blonde hair, thick and wiry, sticks to his forehead. His changing voice sometimes wavers from high to low, wisps of hair sprout in his armpits, and his left eye drifts from a beating he got from his father.

We both live in the Ponce de León housing projects, where my family moved six months ago, and I have a lot of growing up to do. My new friends show me how to steal, lie, cuss, and survive in a simmering working-class neighborhood. The cinderblock buildings built by the government after the War lie in a row like barracks at an army base. The apartments have lawns of tough St. Augustine grass front and back. Bougainvillea vines bloom year-round, hibiscus bushes line the sidewalks, and two old oak trees stand guard outside my bedroom window.

My father's been laid off from his cigar-factory job and he does whatever work he can find. He sells *bolita* numbers for the lottery, works as a janitor in the school system, and still makes cigars at night, in a small *chinchal* in our neighborhood. *Chinchales* are tiny home workshops in someone's shed or garage, so-called because the workers are crowded together like *chinchas* or bedbugs.

After that confrontation with Jesse, I carefully plan my route to and from school to avoid him and other troublemakers. I don't go near the playground where I know they'll be hanging out and smoking cigarettes. In the evenings, I stay in our apartment and listen to *Dragnet, Suspense*, and *Jack Benny* on the radio.

"Why don't you go out and play with your friends, Tony?" my mother says. "It's not right for you to stay at home every night." She's short, with muscular legs, and wears a white cotton apron that smells of garlic.

"Not now, Mom, I have to find out what happens to the Green Hornet."

A week later, I leave the shelter of home to play marbles with Anna and her friends under the streetlamp outside our apartment. We place our marbles in a circle on the sand and line up to shoot.

"Hey Paper Doll, can I play?" It's Jesse and his buddies.

"Sure, if you want to," My voice shakes.

"You're dammed right I want to," he says and scatters the marbles across the hard-packed sand with his feet. The other kids run away but I stay there under the lamppost.

A canopy of bats falls from the moss-laden oak and the dark fuzzy creatures dart in all directions, feasting on swarms of mosquitoes.

"You must be feeling brave tonight, Paper Doll." Jesse gets closer. "Here, have a cigarette," He holds out the soggy pack of *Lucky Strikes* that he carries in his socks.

"Thanks, but I don't smoke." I say.

"Well, it's about time you did," he says, and shoves the unfiltered cigarette into my mouth. He lights a Zippo on his pant leg, and holds the flame to my cigarette.

"Now, breathe, punk. Inhale."

I take in a mouthful of smoke and let it our right away.

"No dummy, not like that. You take a drag, stop, then take another deep breath and swallow the smoke."

I do as he says, and I choke, I can't stop coughing. Jesse and the other guys laugh. I feel a little woozy but I like this new sensation. Then I get dizzy, sweat and feel like throwing up.

"I can't do it, Jesse. Please, let me go."

"I knew you were a homo," He says, and shoves me to the ground. "Now, get the hell out of here. You make me sick."

I run all the way home, lock the doors and close the blinds. I am truly his prisoner. Safe in my bedroom, I read old copies of *Ring* Magazine and books on boxing and wrestling to learn how to defend myself. I do hundreds of pushups every day, and even send away for the Charles Atlas muscle-building course. My body grows harder and stronger, but nothing builds my courage. Fear hangs over me like a thunderhead.

A few weeks later, Jesse comes by again with his buddies while I'm mowing the lawn in our back yard. He stands on the sidewalk a few feet away, hands in his pockets, chewing gum.

"O.K., Paper Doll, go inside now, and you won't get hurt," he says. "Go play with the girls."

But this time, I don't run away. I don't move.

"Maybe you didn't hear me," blusters Jesse, "I said, 'Go inside, kid.'" He kicks the spokes on my shiny Schwinn bike that stands chained to the clothesline post.

I take off my glasses, let my hands hang loose at my side, and wait for him to make the next move. A few neighborhood kids come running to join Jesse's buddies in watching the contest. They form a circle around the two of us as we face off. Jesse fakes a move to one side, then pushes me on the chest with both hands. I slip on the freshly-cut grass and fall on my butt.

"Get up Tony! Get up!" The circled kids yell.

Jesse's neck reddens; sweat drips from his chin. He pauses, spits out his chewing gum. I scramble to my feet, and he punches me with his right fist. It's a wide "John Wayne" swinging punch. I turn my body, deflect the blow and Jesse loses his balance. I don't wait for him recover. I come back instantly with a windmill of fists, blocks and a couple of kicks. I ram my head into his stomach, and knock him breathless. More confident now, I deliver one of my best punches. He ducks his head, and my fist catches him sideways in the mouth. I feel something give. His head spins to the side and one of his teeth lands at our feet.

For a moment we both just stand there, stunned, immobile. Jesse's hands cover his bloody mouth and tears form in his eyes. My knuckles, swollen and cut, throb with each heartbeat.

My mother, who's been watching from the window, comes out and separates us. "Had enough?" she asks Jesse, "Had enough?" she yells at me. She puts her arm around him and he sobs. I've never seen Jesse cry. The kids who came to watch the fight walk away in twos and threes, giggling and shaking their heads. His so-called buddies are long gone. Mom leads Jesse to the porch and wipes his face with a damp washcloth.

"Here," she says, wrapping an ice cube in a clean cloth. "Put this on your mouth until you get home." He walks away without looking up.

My sister runs over, yelling, "You won, Tony! You won!"

I'm not sure what to say. I just stand there smiling, panting for breath. I wipe my nose on my arm. My smile turns to joyful laughter. "Yes. I whipped him!"

"Don't get too cocky, young man. I don't want any more fighting or hitting around here, understand?" My mother says, and goes into the kitchen. When she's gone, I pick up Jesse's tooth and slip it into my pocket.

The next day I go to the playground with no fear and ride my bike all over the neighborhood. I even cruise back and forth in front of Jesse's house. Though I never see him, one of his former buddies asks to hang out with me.

Three days later, Jesse comes to our front door. A yellowed temporary tooth covers the gap in his mouth.

"I'm sorry Paper Doll, I apologize for picking on you." He lowers his eyes.

"Call me Tony from now on," I insist.

"Okay, Tony. I'm sorry." He holds out his hand. "Shake?"

"It's okay, man. Forget it." I say and press the uprooted and blood-caked tooth into his palm.

He stares at it, then roars with laughter. I laugh, too.

"I want to be your friend, Tony," he says. "Let's go fishing on Saturday."

He takes me fishing, buys me my first beer. A week later we clean out my uncle's garage, make two dollars. We get a six-pack of Pabst Blue Ribbon and finish it on the dark bleachers of Cuscaden Park.

"I know what we can do now." He slurs.

"What?" I say, feeling no pain.

"Let's climb the wall into the pool."

We swim underwater in the silence of midnight, intimately exploring each other's bodies. When we get out, we lay naked on the warm concrete deck side by side, head to toe, under a dome of stars. Jesse holds my hand in a gentle grip.

"Listen Tony, I like you a lot. But I want you to promise you'll never tell anyone about this night." He sits up and pulls me to face him. "What do you say, man? Promise?"

"Sure, Jesse. I promise. This can be our private secret."

We stand and he presses his hard body to mine.

"Maybe we can come back here again next weekend?"

"Maybe," I say, and slip into my jeans and tank-top.

Jesse walks me to my bicycle.

A month later, I'm up at two a.m. to start my second job delivering a morning daily, *La Traducion Prensa*, to my neighbors in the Ponce de León Courts. I've bought a new headlamp and rear reflectors for my nighttime rides, and it's an easy route, down sidewalks that form a grid around the two-story apartment buildings. I get to the Jordan household, the last stop on my route, at sunrise.

I don't want to see Jesse. After that night, at Cuscaden Pool, Jesse stopped speaking to me. He ignored me at school, and seemed to be avoiding me altogether.

I coast past their door on my silent Schwinn and lob the paper on the porch.

"Wait up, Tony!" Jesse comes through the door, shirtless, buttoning his jeans. "Where you going, man? I see your basket's empty."

"Nowhere. Just home for coffee."

"I have *coffee* and *pan con mantequilla* already made. Why don't you lock up your bike and come inside?" he says with a crooked smile.

"What about your father?"

"He's in Miami for a week. I'm here alone."

After a coffee and cognac, we do "it" again. This time we romp on his father's bed and it's reciprocal, passionate.

Once more, he stops speaking to me afterwards. And so it goes for the rest of the summer; a stolen moment followed by the silent treatment. When school starts in the fall, he hangs out with a crowd of rowdy older boys and ignores me altogether.

I spend all my free time fishing and forget all about Jesse and our teen romance until my senior year when he and I happen to date the same girl, Stella Golden, a redheaded cheerleader who wears falsies.

"I hear that you and Jesse had lots of fun on your midnight swims," Stella says to me in the school lunchroom. "I wish I could have been there."

STREETCAR

I point my Brownie Hawkeye camera at my mother and sister, who stand arm-in-arm on the sidewalk next to the streetcar tracks. They smile, I snap. Mother is wearing a white cotton low-cut dress and a wide-brimmed hat. She looks like Vivian Leigh in *Gone with the Wind*.

My sister, Anita, is in dungarees and a baggy T-shirt to hide her fully formed boobs; I've seen them. She's captain of the high school softball team and we're going downtown a week before Christmas to buy her a uniform. I'm getting a pair of gym shorts and a jockstrap for P.E. class. I hate shopping. I especially hate shopping with my mother. She gets into arguments over the price, or the service, or asks to see the manager. She's always embarrassing me.

The noon streetcar glides to a stop just past 22nd Street, twenty minutes late. All the passengers get off and scatter in every direction. This local streetcar line shuttles back and forth between Ybor City and downtown Tampa all day. At each end of the route, the motorman, a short, bowlegged man with lots of hair, shuts the doors, moves the coin-box to the other end of the streetcar, then walks down the aisle flipping all the seat-backs to face in the opposite direction. Next, he steps outside and reaches through the window to close the doors. He lowers the trolley and secures it to the hook, then heads for the Columbia Restaurant across the street.

"Where are you going, Mister?" Mother yells from the sidewalk. "My kids and I need to get downtown, we're already a half-hour late."

"Forgive me, *Senora*, but nature calls, I have to relieve myself first," his eyes scan my mother head to toe. "You want to give me a hand?" He touches his crotch.

"Get your mother to give you a hand, you worm. And please show more respect. I may be a widow, but I'm not a whore."

He howls in laughter and darts through the swinging doors into the cantina.

"Ma, why is that man laughing?" Anita asks.

"Because he's stupid, that's why, like most men."

"Mama, can we get on the streetcar? I want to drive it!" I tug on her dress.

"If that idiot can drive a streetcar, son, anybody can. His name is Raul. He dated my cousin, Dora. She said he's a lousy lover and belongs to the Klan."

Raul returns, carrying a glass of *café con leche,* and boards the streetcar. Passengers crowd at the door. Anita and I get on first. My mother trips on the top step and Raul jumps from his seat to catch her. But she pushes him away.

"I don't need your help, Mr. Conductor."

"I'm so sorry for the delay, Madam. Had I known what a beautiful woman you are I would have rushed to get you downtown"

"Stash it, Mister; I'm not interested in dwarfs." She drops the money into the coin box and asks for three transfers.

"I'm sorry Senora, but that's not a dime, it's a penny." He smiles and stares at my mother's breasts.

She peers into the glass coin box. "What do you mean, not a dime?"

"That's right. It's one of those new 1943 pennies made out of zinc. The copper is needed to fight the war against the Japs."

"This capitalist war will be the ruin of us all." She pays the fare.

"Remember Pearl Harbor," he chimes in.

My sister and I run down the wood-planked aisle past dozens of passengers and take seats near the rear of the car. Anita sits astride two seats with one foot propped up on the windowsill. I sit behind her on the aisle. In the viewfinder of my tiny camera, the inside of the car looks like a spaceship; brass fittings, steel bars on the windows, teakwood molding and rattan seats.

Mother follows us to the rear of the car. "Anita, sit up straight. And, cross your legs." She takes off her hat. Her long auburn hair spills to her shoulders. "I'll make a young lady out of you yet." She sits down next to Anita, kicks off her shoes and sighs.

"I'm sorry, Senora, but you can't sit there," Raul speaks into the rear-view mirror.

My mother doesn't move.

"You can't sit there, Madam. That's the colored section. White passengers must sit in the front of the car."

"Do I look white to you?"

A few of the Negro passengers turn around and look at her.

"For all you know, Romeo, I'm not white."

Two colored ladies roll their eyes.

"I could be a *mulatta*, or an octoroon."

"Look lady, I don't care if you're an octopus, this streetcar is not moving until you and the children move up into the white section."

In Florida all public facilities are segregated; water fountains for whites only, others for coloreds. White toilets, black toilets; restaurants serve only whites in the dining room. Coloreds can buy food only at the back window, and passengers on public buses and streetcars are seated according to race.

"These folks are just as good as us, Raul. Why should they have to sit in the back of the streetcar?"

"How do you know my name?

"I'm Cristina. Dora's cousin."

"Dora? Oh my God, a vision of heaven." His eyes glaze. "I miss her so much."

He turns to the front, trips the magneto switch and the streetcar begins to move. "You can stay there for now, Cristina, but when we get to Fifteenth Street, you have to move up front or take another car."

I sit at the window and look out at *La Setima,* Ybor City's main shopping district. Christmas shoppers are everywhere, at the department stores, five-and-dime, restaurants and coffee shops. A ten-foot Santa smiles at children from the windows of Spicola Hardware. A blue spruce reaches the ceiling at The Latin American Bank.

21st Street, no more stops until Eighteenth. The streetcar speeds up; the giant electric motors strain. I see a blur of business signs: The Silver Dollar Café, Agliano's Fish Market, F. Leto and Son Grocery, and La Tropicana, a deviled-crab and Cuban-sandwich place where locals gather to drink *café con leche* and gossip.

The streetcar comes to a full stop at Eighteenth. The doors part; more passengers get on. They stare at the three whites sitting in the colored section. Some giggle, but most of them frown. One black woman mistakenly takes a seat in the white section, but is quickly corrected by her friends. My mother busies herself braiding my sister's hair. Out of my window I see the majestic Italian Club, with its cantina, ballrooms, and a cinema called the Broadway, where on Saturday mornings I can see cartoons, Flash Gordon serials, and a Hopalong Cassidy western for nine cents.

"Fifteenth Street, next stop!" Raul yells, staring directly at my mother in the mirror. An older negro man runs to catch the streetcar; Raul slams the door in his face, and laughs.

I get a snapshot of Buchman's department store across the street. They sell almost anything you want: clothes, shoes, camping and fishing gear, Army surplus and jeans. When I was in the fourth grade, I tried to sell Mrs. Buchman a ticket to the school's May Festival.

"Can colored people go there?" she asked.

"No, I don't think so. But you're not colored."

"Yes I am. I'm a Jew."

Raul guns the streetcar and we speed past El Centro Español, an ornate red-brick building that houses a *cantina*, ballrooms, and a movie theater, the Casino, where my father would take me to see Spanish-language movies, Mexican *corridos* with Jorge Negrete, the Singing Cowboy, or melodramas with Sylvia Pinal. Shoppers throng to Kress's, Penney's, and Thom McCann. Salvation Army kettles hang outside Fernandez y Garcia. Hungry shoppers line up at the Buen Gusto for a bowl of Spanish bean soup.

The streetcar crosses Fifteenth Street and slams to a sudden stop in front of Las Novedades—Raul dropped the brake blocks too soon. Standing passengers swing on straps and grumble as they disembark to connect with other streetcar and bus lines. Only two Negro women wearing almost identical feathered hats now remain in the car with the three of us.

Raul combs his hair, puts on his motorman's jacket, and marches down the aisle to where we sit. He looks taller in uniform, his face fixed in a frown. I take a flash picture of him in his cowboy boots. He blinks.

"Listen, Cristina, move to the front now or get off." His body is stiff, his shoulders back. The two Negro women leave quietly by the front door. "I could lose my job over your bullshit."

"I'm not moving anywhere, big boy. You guys in uniform think you own this country but you're wrong. When working-class people like me stand up for our rights, you'll be left behind naked and without a badge." She crosses her legs, looks out the window. My sister and I sink into our seats.

"That's it, Cristina. I've heard enough of your Communist bullshit. I'm calling the police." He picks up the coin box and leaves the car but sticks his head back in. "People like you belong in camps," he yells.

"Fascist pig!" my mother snarls, standing at mid-aisle, hands on hips.

Raul's face turns deep red. He runs to the Ritz Theater to use the pay phone in the lobby and leaves the car doors open, the motor running, and the trolley engaged.

My mother dashes to the front of the car and drops into the motorman's seat. She pulls the lever to close the doors, raises the block brakes, sounds the horn, and the car inches forward silently, propelled only by gravity.

"Mother, what are you doing? Are you crazy?" Anita yells. "You'll get us killed."

"No I won't, darling, all I have to do is follow the tracks." She flips the magneto, pushes the throttle and nothing happens. She slams it with her fist and the streetcar lunges forward and travels west on Seventh Avenue at a fast clip.

I run to the back of the car. Through my viewfinder I see Raul do a double-take as he glances up from his irate phone call. He drops the receiver and comes running after us, howling for my mother to stop, his short legs pumping comically. I snap his picture as he falls to his knees in frustrated exhaustion, shaking his fists and no doubt cursing. I run back up to the front.

"Way to go, Mom! This is really fun! Can I drive now?" I ask.

"Not yet, son. Let me get the hang of it first." I snap a photo of her at the controls. She looks at the camera, smiles, and clangs the bell.

We glide past Avenida Republica de Cuba, Thirteeth Street, Twelfth Street. Jaywalkers scatter, and autos pull over at the sound of the horn and the speeding streetcar. We run the red light at Eleventh Street.

"Please slow down, Mom. I'm scared," Anita whimpers.

At Nebraska Avenue the tracks make a sharp left turn. The streetcar hits the curve too fast and leans to the right. The wheels leave the rails and slice across the pavement, creating a wave of sparks. The trolley jumps the wire and the pole flaps around like an injured cobra, zapping everything it strikes, One of the motors catches fire, and a plume of smoke rises above the rooftops, just as a squadron of police cars arrives on the scene.

No one is hurt. The three of us are shook up, but OK.

Anita and I are chauffeured to our grandmother's house in a police car. Mother is treated for minor burns on her hands and booked at the City Jail. She's charged with grand theft, destruction of government property, reckless driving, endangering the lives of minors, and resisting arrest. Her bail is set at five hundred dollars.

In a dream I see my mother, handcuffed, walking down a dark hallway to the electric chair. I awake sobbing. Sometimes, I think the angels in heaven made a mistake and delivered my soul to the wrong house.

The next day, I go to the City Jail to see Mother. Anita wouldn't come; she hates cops. No one in our family can post the bail; $500 is a year's wages for them. I've brought her a snapshot I took of the derailed streetcar firmly grounded ten feet away from a gasoline storage tank.

The Jail is directly behind City Hall, next to Police Headquarters. I open the heavy doors and walk up to the desk. A fake Christmas tree with no lights sits in the corner.

"Can I see my Mother?" I ask the bailiff.

"What's your mother's name?" he asks squinting at me.

"Cristina. Cristina Martinez," a man's voice announces from the waiting room.

It's Raul. What's he doing here?

"Your mother will be out of jail in a few minutes, son. I just paid her bail." He puffs out his chest, hitches up his pants.

The steel door leading to the cellblock slides open and my mother steps through, wearing a pin-striped prison uniform and rubber sneakers. I run and throw my arms around her waist. She kisses my head.

"Thank you, Don Raul, for posting my bail." Mother extends her hand. "But why did you do it? And where did you get the money?"

"I was wrong, Cristina. I just could not leave well enough alone." He takes a deep breath. "I'm sorry. This whole thing was my fault." He looks directly into her eyes. "Last night I decided I could not leave a beautiful woman like you wasting away in jail." He clears his throat. "Cristina, I think I'm in love with you."

"In love?" She rolls her eyes. "But we just met, Raul. I know nothing about you."

He pulls out a savings passbook. "I have five thousand dollars in this bank account, my house is paid for, I have friends in high places and I own a forty-four pistol. That boy of yours could use a new pair of shoes and your daughter needs teeth work."

He takes her hand and drops to one knee.

"Cristina, I'm a sucker for a woman of passion. Will you marry me?"

For once Mother is speechless. She looks at me, wide-eyed, mouth open. I almost laugh, but instead I look at my feet. I want those new shoes.

She looks at the bailiff and he nods, "Yes. Yes."

Raul is still on one knee.

"I'm truly honored, Raul," she begins. "But things are moving too fast for me, I need time to think it over."

"Hallelujah!" he kisses her hand. "That wasn't a 'no.' Let's get out of here. I have a taxi waiting."

I aim my Nikon M. 35mm camera at Raul and my mother, who are eating hot dogs at the picnic table in Ballast Point Park. This camera, which Raul bought for me at a pawnshop, has a high-speed shutter and a combined view- and range-finder. He also bought me the shoes he promised and a catcher's mitt for Anita, but she refuses to accept any gifts from him.

It's been three months since Raul bailed Mother out of jail and hired a local Italian attorney to defend her. She got off lightly; one year's probation, no jail time, and she won't have to pay damages to the government.

"Christina, I'm a patient man and I love you very much, but I'm getting tired of waiting for your answer." He dips into the potato salad.

"I told you, I need to think it over." She looks out across the Bay at the giant freighters sailing into Port Tampa. "It's hard for me to turn my back on my dead husband."

"I'm sure he was a wonderful man, but please think about the future. When you marry me you'll live in my big house on Palm Avenue, have a full-time housekeeper, and you won't have to work."

"I'm not interested in being anybody's wife, Raul." She places more wieners on the grill.

"My relatives think I'm crazy to pursue a Cuban cigar-maker's daughter, but I love you so much, Christina. I just want you to live with me."

"Now that's a different story." She walks around to his side of the table and massages his shoulders. "You know *querido*, living together is not the same thing as marriage. Lovers stay together because they want to, not because the law or your relatives say we have to. Is that what you want?" Her hands slide down his chest; he looks up and they kiss. I capture the moment on celluloid film.

NIGHT FISHING

I'm sleeping over at my friend Fernando's tonight. We share a single bed, and I can't fall asleep. I listen to his rhythmic breathing, smell his musky skin, and sense the heat from his naked body. No use fighting it; I'm aroused. He rolls over and drapes his arm around me. He doesn't wake up. Then he throws one leg around my knees and draws me close to his bony body. In the morning we awake in the same position.

"What kind of sandwiches are you making?" I ask in his mother's kitchen.

"The usual: baloney, cheese and mustard on Holsom Bread. What kind have you got, Julio?" He doesn't look at me.

"Same as always; egg tortilla and onion on Cuban bread."

He lines up a dozen slices of white bread and piles on the ingredients. I stand next to him. I wonder if he remembers our closeness last night.

"Did you bring the work gloves?" He shatters the morning silence in his newly-deep man's voice.

"Yes, I bought four pairs at Spicola's."

"Well, don't just stand there, pack them in the tackle box. We have a lot of work to do today."

His unsmiling face ignites me into a protest: "Hey man, get off my back."

His body stiffens. He clenches a shiny knife in his hand. He lowers his head and takes a deep breath.

"I'm sorry, Julio. It's not about you; it's about my father. He came home yesterday after a three-day binge and tore up all my drawings, even the pencil portrait I did of you in sixth grade. He said I need to concentrate on schoolwork not on these sissy pictures. Then he threatened to beat me again."

"Where is your father now?"

"At the *cantina* drinking his morning cognac. He'll be home soon; let's load the bikes and get the hell out of here."

I'd just turned fourteen when I met Fernando Fernandez in the junior high P.E. class. A whiz at basketball, he never made the team because he didn't show up for practice. The other kids thought Fernando was weird. He never took part in teen activities, spent a lot of time alone, and behaved more like an adult than a fifteen-year old. A mop of red hair capped his six-foot frame and spilled down over his ears and eyes. Last week in the boys' shower I saw big red welts on his back and legs.

One day, on my way home from school, Fernando asked me to go fishing. I'd never fished before, but jumped at the chance to be with him. We fished at Robles Park Lake, using a short piece of fishing line, a tiny hook, and bubblegum for bait. We landed two catfish and three small sunfish and released them. I felt a new thrill in matching wits with these unseen creatures of the deep.

Almost every weekend after that, Fernando and I went fishing all over Tampa Bay—the causeway, Davis Islands, Hillsboro River, and the banana docks where we cast our lures alongside giant ocean freighters. Tonight we hope to land a big silver tarpon on a thick hand-line, using a six-inch Eagle Claw hook baited with half a chicken.

We pedal ten miles from Ybor City to Ballast Point in record time. We wind past the shipping docks, along the waterfront and across the Platt Street Bridge to Bay Shore Boulevard, a wide palm-lined avenue that hugs the coastline in a five-mile crescent. The setting sun casts a red glow on the water. From here I can see a silhouette of the fishing pier floating on the horizon.

We chain our bikes in Jules Verne Park next to the pier. In Verne's novel, *Journey to the Moon,* the rocket takes off from Tampa Village, perhaps from the very spot where today sprawls an ancient banyan tree. An old wooden building at the foot of the pier houses a snack bar and a residence for Ramon, the caretaker, and his family. Fernando and I lug all our tackle, plus 200 yards of tarpon line, through the snack bar and out the back door to the pier.

"Isn't it a little late for you boys?" Ramon asks.

"Not at all, Don Ramon," Fernando replies. "The tide's coming in, it's getting dark, and tarpon feed at night."

"Julio, does your mother know you're going night fishing?"

"Yes sir," I reply, and look away.

Ramon puts his hand on my shoulder. "Well, be careful; it might storm tonight. Did you hear about the shark attack at the Causeway?"

"No. What happened?" Fernando asks, wide-eyed.

"A nine-foot shark shredded a diver's foot. It took over 100 stitches to sew him up."

"Humans don't taste good to sharks," Fernando says. "They take one bite and spit us out."

"If you need any help, just yell," Ramon adds, and disappears into the kitchen.

We set up our lines halfway down the pier on the boat dock near water level. Only amateurs and tourists fish under the roofed shelter at the pier's end. Fernando picks up the baited tarpon line, circles it over his head like a lasso, and casts it out into the night. He wraps the manila rope around a tall bamboo pole topped with a cowbell, and winds the loose end around a railing.

An hour goes by and not much happens, just nibbles from pinfish. The tarpon line is dead in the water. The wind shifts to the west; whitecaps frost the Bay. I hook something that stretches my line and cuts through the water. After a brief fight I land a two-pound stingray. My hook is buried in his wing.

"Fabulous," says Fernando. "Now we have the right bait." He hauls in the tarpon line, replaces the chicken with the live stingray, and tosses it back into the choppy water. "Come and get it," he yells.

The only other person on the pier is Sheep Head John, a master fisherman. Others copy him, but he always manages to catch the most fish. Waiting is a big part of fishing, and John can wait forever. No one knows how old he is; he's always short of breath, smokes cigars, and drinks a lot of beer.

"Let's eat; I'm starving," Fernando says, and unpacks his sandwiches on the wooden bench built into the railing.

I sit next to him. He looks down at me, and smiles. I want to hold his hand.

Heavy clouds move in and cover most of the sky. I smell rain in the air. I eat my stiff sandwiches in silence and stare at the baited lines in the water.

"You know, Julio, this may be the last time we go fishing together."

"The last time? Why?" My heart races.

"I'm leaving home. I can't live with my father any more. He's drinks every day now. Last week when I was in school he gave my mother a black eye and a bloody lip. I'm afraid if I stay, I'll have to kill him."

"You can't leave home; you're not even sixteen."

"Who cares? I can take care of myself. I have a bus ticket to Key West on Thursday, and enough money for two nights in a motel. I'll lie about my age and get a job on a shrimp boat. No one will ever find me."

"What about our plan to go trout fishing in Ozona next weekend? I can't go without you."

"Yes you can, you're almost a man now." He puts his hand on my knee. "Listen Julio, I want you to know that I'm different from you. I like girls." His eyes follow the tarpon line rising and falling with the swells. "But none of that bullshit matters. You'll always be my best friend."

My mouth fills with saliva. I swallow hard.

"Please don't go away, Fernando. You're my only real friend."

Fernando stands. "I'll be right back," he says. "I'm going to the snack bar to get some sodas before it rains."

Dark rain-clouds lined in silver hide the quarter moon hanging over Palmetto Beach. I can't stop thinking about what Fernando said. He knows I like boys. One day he walked in on Harry Alvarez and me fooling around in the boys' showers. Is that why he's leaving? I try to quiet the turmoil in my head by casting my lure over and over into the indigo waters.

The jangle of the cowbell awakens me. I drop my rod and try to grab the tarpon line but it plays out like a wild tornado. Raindrops strike me in the face. Half our line is gone and the fish is still running. Where the hell is Fernando? Oh shit, I can't believe it; the end of the line is not secured, just wrapped around the railing. I move as fast as I can on the wet deck, pull the rope free, wind it around a steel bollard, and tie a series of half-hitches around a concrete piling.

"Your gloves, Julio! Put on your gloves!" Fernando comes running. "I'll get the ponchos." The wind shifts to southeast; thunder rumbles overhead.

"This is no tarpon," he says. "A tarpon would have jumped by now."

We grasp the line with our gloved hands and try to slow it down but before long all 200 yards are in the water. The pull of the fish makes the pier move. I can hear the taut line slicing through the dark waters but can't see it. The hooked creature swims back and forth fighting to get free. Knots tied around the piling squeak. We take in some slack but the fish makes another run for it. I can't stop the line; it's going out too fast. My gloves fray, and I feel the wooden planks shift under my feet.

"Cut the line. Release it." Sheep Head John yells from down the pier. "You boys are no match for that monster."

"No way, Sir," Fernando holds tight to the line. "This is the biggest fish I've ever hooked. I want to see what it looks like."

"Well, you're doing it wrong," John says. "You can't muscle a fish this big. Take in only as much line as you can hold. Wrap it around this beam and tighten the coil each time you pull in some slack. It's slow going, but you won't lose any ground." He turns and heads for the snack bar. "I'll get some help."

More rain-clouds move in. Thunder crackles overhead. Lightning strikes a utility pole and the lights on the pier go out. Fernando hands me a flashlight. "Here, baby, keep it aimed at the line." He winks at me.

Ten minutes later, Ramon arrives out of breath, carrying a gaff in one hand and a rifle in the other.

"Looks like you boys have your hands full," Ramon says. "Let me play with this monster." Fernando hands him the line.

Just then the fish stops fighting. It makes a big circle and swims towards the pier. The line slackens and floats on the water. We scramble to gather in the wet manila rope and secure it. The fish swims under the pier and stops running. I can see a gray shadow, like a ghost treading water below the surface. We inch in the line and the first thing I see is the dorsal fin of a shark.

"Nurse shark," Ramon says, shining a flashlight under the pier. "A female, and she's pregnant."

We take in more line, and the shark's head bobs to the surface. Her tail swishes from side to side; blood trails from her puckered mouth lined with rows of razor-sharp teeth. She's exhausted. Her gills barely move and her eyes have no pupils. She looks oddly peaceful.

"Keep her head out of the water, Fernando; I'll put an end to this struggle." Ramon loads a cartridge of shells into his rifle.

"No, Don Ramon. Please don't shoot. Julio and I want to land her alive, we'll never have a chance like this again."

Ramon hesitates, and then puts down the gun. "O.K. She's all yours. I'll go set up the winch, bring her there. But remember, move slowly; no slack."

I take my turn at walking the shark alongside the pier, as if on a short leash. Fernando leapfrogs ahead and ties the line to the next post. I've never seen him so happy. He stops, cuts his eyes at me, and grins. I nod and smile.

Fernando walks the shark for the final ten yards. Ramon grasps the leader cable and hooks it up to the winch. The electric motor strains as it raises our catch out of the water.

"Wow! At least 400 pounds!" says Sheep Head John.

Suddenly the shark stiffens, arches her body, and whips her tail with terrific force. The cable snaps. She drops into the water, splashing all of us standing on the pier. The shark is now free to swim away, but for some reason she can't dive. She floats aimlessly on the surface with her nose out of the water.

"Grab the leader. Gaff her," Fernando yells.

"No need for that, son," says Ramon. "She broke her backbone doing that last trick. She'll die soon and float to shore."

Ramon uses a block-and-tackle to hang the carcass on the scale. The shark's tail curls on the deck. "She has to be bled, or the flesh won't be any good to eat." He draws a hooked butcher knife from his belt and jams the sharp point just above the shark's anus and cuts open her gut. He's still cutting when the first spotted pup wiggles out and lands on the deck, followed by another and then another.

I stifle a scream and start to cry. Fernando puts his arm around me, pulls my sobbing head to his chest and holds me. I can't stop shaking.

Ramon looks at Sheep Head John and they smile.

"Come inside, boys. I'll get you some dry clothes and fix you a hamburger. It's time to go home. Maybe next weekend you'll catch that tarpon, Fernando."

"That would be great, Ramon, but next weekend Julio and I are going trout fishing in Ozona." He holds my hand.

EL LECTOR

Abel, his tanned skin glistening, picked up the splintered planks and tossed them on the horse-drawn wagon backed up to the factory loading dock. He had stayed home from school that day to help his Uncle Julian pick up the pieces of the *lector*'s platform that had been destroyed by thugs hired by the cigar-factory owners. Abel's muscled body easily loaded most of the lumber; beside him, Julian worked slowly and silently, caressing each board as if it were an old friend, a chapter from one of his novels.

Every day for the past twenty years, Julian stood on that raised platform in the middle of the factory floor, reading to the workers: *Anna Karenina, War and Peace, Les Miserables,* writings of Cervantes, newspapers, and the poems of José Marti. He didn't just read the words; he took on the voice and mannerisms of the characters in the novels, like an actor in the theater. Good performances were followed by the sustained thumping roar of two hundred *chavetas,* or tobacco knives, repeatedly striking the workers' tobacco-cutting boards.

"What are you going to do now, Uncle Julian?" Abel asked, tossing the final plank on the wagon.

"Who knows? Maybe I can still find a *lector*'s position in New Orleans or Key West."

"Can I come with you?"

"*Lo siento*, Abel, but your mother would miss you too much." The lunchtime whistle blew and cigar-makers swarmed out of the factory like bees abandoning a hive.

Julian roped the final boards to the wagon, paid the driver, and wheeled his bicycle to the curb. His sweat-soaked shirt, usually pristine and starched, hung limply on his slim frame. A stray ocean breeze squeezed through the humid summer air and rustled the magnolia trees.

"I'm grateful to have a night job at the Cantina." He raised the kickstand on his English bicycle. "I saw it coming. I could smell the wolf at the door."

"What wolf, *Tio*?"

"Who else? Those blood-sucking factory owners from Spain. They said that my readings of Russian novels and revolutionary newspapers put crazy ideas into the workers' heads and created unrest. Over the past two months, all *lector*s have been locked out of the factories and replaced with radios playing music, local news, and commercials. My neighbor's father, a Mexican, shot and killed one of these arrogant Spaniards in a duel fair and square, but afterwards he was locked out of the cigar factories, just like me. It's not over yet, and I'm afraid things are going to get violent." An electric streetcar rattled down Michigan Avenue, headed for downtown Tampa.

Julian's sharp Spanish nose, thick eyebrows and gentle manner attracted many lady friends, but he remained a solitary bird. He spent a lot of time with his best friend, Tito Jimenez, an avid labor organizer, artist, and graduate of the University of Havana. I liked Tito, a stocky man with a mop of curly hair and short legs that caused him to walk with a shuffle.

Together, the two men read novels in their original languages, spent hours in Tito's darkroom printing photos, and at high tide on moonlit nights they fished for snook under the Buffalo Avenue Bridge. Julian had never owned an automobile and never wanted one. He could be seen pedaling his bicycle to work every morning at six a.m., always neatly dressed, with a starched shirt, tie, and straw hat.

One hot night a week later, Abel walked through swarms of mosquitoes and lightning bugs to his grandparents' house. Julian, who lived in a studio room at the rear of the house, invited him in. They stood in the doorway, both of them about the same height, both with tall angular bodies that moved with a gentleness not usually found in other men. They sat by the screen door, Julian knitting a cast net that he was making for Tito, and Abel mending his uncle's shirts with a sharp needle and thread.

"Are the boys in school still picking on you?" Julian asked his nephew gently.

"Not any more," replied Abel. He put down his sewing and stood up, puffing out his chest a little. "Last spring one kid punched me and called me a sissy and a homo, but I did some training and exercising during the summer, and the next time he tried to hit me, I gave him a bloody nose; no trouble since then." He dropped into a boxer's stance and faked a couple of punches.

"Good for you," Julian nodded approvingly, "You can't let anybody push you around. What are you going to do after graduation?"

"Go to the university and study theatre arts, drama and dance. When I was little, I wanted to be a clown when I grew up."

"Clowning won't get you many jobs. What else can you do?"

"I'd be great backstage." Abel paced across the room, his skinny arms punctuating every phrase like a politician, "I can sew on a treadle or electric sewing machine, I can build sets, I know how to cook, iron, and clean house. My mother, aunt and sisters trained me very well."

"So you want to be an actor?"

"Yes *Tio*, I want to make people laugh and cry just like you do."

"Well, there's certainly no future in becoming a *lector*." Julian poured two shots of cognac. "*Lectors* will disappear just like the dinosaurs."

"Not you *Tio*, you are the best."

"*Salud*," they raised their glasses. "To you, Abel; may you have a long career on the stage. And, remember, be yourself, no matter what anybody else thinks."

The following week, the cigar-makers went on strike and organized a boycott of downtown Tampa merchants. Tito, who was a seasoned activist, marched in the demonstrations, Julian beside him. After sunset, the mob set cars aflame. Police used dogs, hoses, and billy-clubs against the demonstrators.

No one was killed, but Tito came home with a gash on his forehead, and Julian ended up in jail, charged with subversive activity. The cigar-makers took up a collection for his bail, but the authorities would not release him until the strike was settled and the workers returned to their benches.

When Julian got out of jail, he was suddenly very busy, distributing leaflets, organizing rallies, selling the *Communist Daily Worker* on the doorstep of the cigar factories, and organizing the truck drivers that served the cigar industry.

Abel missed the long talks he used to have with his uncle. He sat alone on the deserted softball bleachers in Cascaden Park, watching a flaming sunset silhouette a row of royal palms on Fifteenth Street.

"*Que pasa, mi amigo*? You look a little *triste*." It was Tito.

"It's *Tio* Julian. He doesn't have time for me anymore."

Listen, Abelito . . ."

"I'm not a kid anymore; please, Tito, call me Abel."

"Okay, Abel; what has happened is that Julian's time in jail turned him into a true revolutionary, a champion of the workers. Today, his trained voice inspires cigar-makers at the Centro Obrero to demand higher wages, better working conditions and a five-day work week."

"But what about his family? His friends?"

"Please try to understand, Abel. In jail, Julian was tortured by the police and physically abused by his cellmates. He's a changed man." A wind-funnel touched down in the infield and raised a twisting column of dust into the thick August air.

That night after midnight, Abel slipped out of bed, got dressed, and walked under a moonless sky to his grandparents' house. From the alley, he saw a dim light burning in Julian's room. The shades were down. He stood outside the bathroom window and heard Tito's voice, but the words got lost in Julian's laughter. Sounds of scuffling followed, then whispers. And after a long silence, the lights went out.

On the night of August 25, 1932, cigar-makers in straw hats, and truck drivers in coveralls and leather caps filled every seat in the Centro Obrero. A line stretched down Ninth Avenue. They had come to listen to Don Julian Fernandez-Blanco, former *lector* and now a representative of the International Workers' Party. Petitions to certify the new truck—drivers' union circulated in the hall.

Tito had invited Abel to the rally and they sat in the first row.

"Where is *Tio* Julian? I haven't seen him all evening."

"He's probably huddling with the union bosses."

"He left home early. I didn't see his bicycle outside."

"Don't worry, Abel. When these opening speakers are done, Julian will appear and set this hall on fire with his oratory."

Just before intermission, an official of the Centro Obrero announced in a booming voice: "*Senoras y Senores*, I deeply regret to inform you that tonight's rally is cancelled. Don Julian, along with Miguel Otero, our esteemed union president, is missing and cannot be located. We've been asked by the police to join in a manhunt of Ybor City to find them."

They did not find the two missing men that night. Nor the next day, nor the next year. With the passing of each day, Tito's spirits sank. Soon he started drinking whiskey and staying home from work. Abel busied himself reconstructing the *lector's* platform in Julian's backyard with the salvaged lumber that seemed to echo with his uncle's voice. Later on, he would use that sacred stage to produce puppet shows for the neighborhood children.

His mother and aunt wore black veils for years and often took flowers to the spot in Palmetto Beach where Julian's bicycle had been found. The authorities said the two men had simply disappeared, and the case was closed.

"*Hola*, Abel, it's me!" Tito's voice crackled over the long-distance lines.

"Tito, *mi compadre*! What a surprise. Why are you calling me after all this time?"

"I wanted to tell you before you read about it in the newspaper. It's taken ten years, but I think we finally have a clue as to what happened to Julian and Otero."

Abel's heart drummed. He pressed the receiver to his ear with both hands.

"Yesterday, a shrimp-boat captain from Palmetto Beach, in jail for black-market activities, confessed that, one night in August 1932, he transported four male passengers to a remote sandbar west of the Marquesas. Two of the men were plainclothes policemen. The other two were bound and gagged, with feed sacks over their heads."

Tito choked and began to cry. The phone line went silent. Then he continued in a scratchy whisper: "Julian and Otero were unloaded on a deserted beach with no water, no food, and no chance of escape. Swimming to the mainland against the currents of the Gulf Stream is impossible. They were left there to die."

"We've got to find them, Tito."

"Too late for that, Abel. The Coast Guard captain in Key West said sandbars near the Gulf Stream come and go at the whim of the currents; there's no hope of finding them alive after all these years."

Abel swallowed, took a deep breath. "And how are you doing, Tito?"

"Much better than the last time you saw me. I left my wife and rented your uncle's old room. Maybe I can't be with Julian anymore, but I can be around his books, his tools, his clothes. And I get to sleep in the bed we shared. Julian is the only man I've ever loved." Tito paused, obviously holding back tears, then asked, more brightly: "How about you, Abel?"

"I'm happier than I've ever been, Tito. I'm so glad I left Ybor City; I could never be myself there. Here in Miami I'm enrolled in the drama department of the University and I live with a wonderful man. He's fifteen years older, and we're very much in love. He reminds me a lot of Julian."

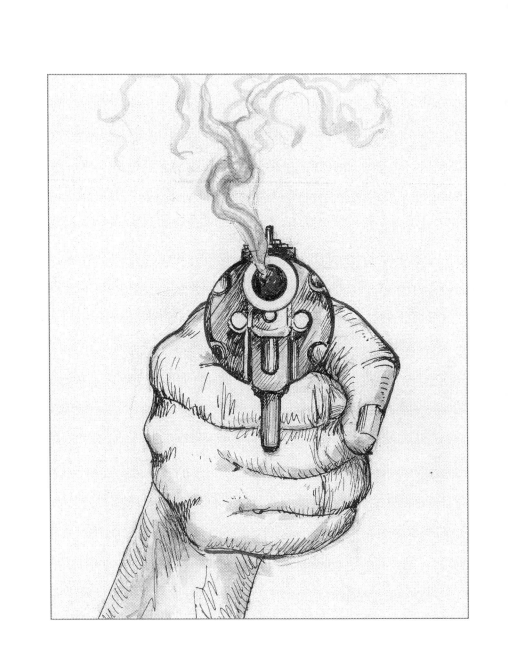

CHUCHO AND SAL

"Did you bring the gun?"

"Yes sir, a forty-four pistol, fully loaded." Chucho draws the blue-steel weapon from his shoulder holster.

"Good. Place it on the table, barrel pointing out. Now, state your full name, age, birthplace, occupation and next of kin," says the referee. He's dressed in black and wearing a bowler.

"*Me llamo* Jesus "Chucho" Sanchez. I'm forty-two. I was born in Michoacán, Mexico, and I've been a cigar-maker at Villason and Company for fifteen years." Chucho brushes his straight black hair away from his chiseled face. Although his stature is short, his strong body is muscled from hard work.

A black sedan approaches around the sand dunes and rumbles to a stop. The driver opens the passenger door for Sal, who steps out into the freezing January morning in his long leather boots and wool coat. He's a tall, broad-shouldered Spaniard who strides into the gathering like a conquistador.

"*Buenos dias*, Senor Fernandez. Please place your weapon on the table. We must inspect both guns to make sure they're working."

"With pleasure," Sal says, and takes the gun from a velvet-lined box that his driver is holding like a tray of appetizers.

"This trusty thirty-eight has never failed me yet." He places the loaded gun on the table and turns to face the small crowd of men who have come out to a deserted Rocky Point Beach at six in the morning to witness a duel.

"My name is Salvador Fernandez; they call me "Sal." I'm fifty-six, born in Galicia, and my wife, Lydia, is my next of kin." He strokes his vest with polished fingernails.

"And you, Chucho, who is your next of kin?" asks the referee.

"I don't have any family" replies Chucho stoically. "I'm an orphan."

Chucho and Sal had worked side by side on the top floor of Villason and Company for fifteen years. Like most of the Spaniards in Ybor City, Sal looked down on Cubans and Mexicans. Although almost everyone detested the Spaniards, a mutual love of soccer had brought Chucho and Sal together.

"You know, Chucho, I don't see what these Cubans see in baseball," Sal would say. "I think Americans invented it to be different from the rest of the world. Baseball players just stand in the outfield fondling their crotches, not like the warriors of soccer who run, kick and bat the ball with their head for hours." Every Monday they scanned the scores of European and Latin American soccer leagues in *La Traducion Prensa* and loyally followed their favorite teams in the race for the World Cup.

In the evening, after dinner, Ybor City's male population hung out in their many social clubs, drank coffee and cognac, played dominoes, and discussed politics and the state of the world. Sal sponsored Chucho's membership in El Centro Español, an exclusive club for the Spanish and those with Spanish blood. His *Gallego* buddies, from Galacia in Spain, didn't like a Mexican in their midst. The two friends met at the club almost every night for coffee and conversation, but soon things got very complicated.

One night, Sal invited Chucho to his house for dinner and introduced his friend to his young wife, Lydia, a lovely young woman with snow-white skin, red lips and blue-black hair brushed into a bun. She had baked a red snapper, steamed yellow rice and fried plantains for dinner.

"Tell me, Chucho," she said. "Which one of these Ybor City beauties are you courting?"

"Not for me," he replied politely, "I like the single life." He tried not to look at her. "How long have you two been married?"

"Ten years; yesterday was our anniversary. I remember when Sal returned to Galicia to meet me; I had just I turned fifteen. We were married in the small Catholic chapel in our village. My father gave me away." She pressed two tobacco-stained fingers to her lips and lowered her long lashes.

"Forgive me, *querida*," Sal interjected. "But your father didn't exactly give you away. I deeded him five acres of the richest farmland in the valley, plus two of my best mules, and I promised to bring you to America."

"This isn't America!" She stood up. "Living in Ybor City is like living in the slums of Havana." She marched to the kitchen, her high heels clacking on the pinewood floor.

Chucho was instantly smitten by this lovely and passionate creature. He managed to hide his feelings from Sal, but not from Lydia. By the time dessert came, she had made eye contact with him and he was hopelessly in love.

A year later, heated words about the merits of Emile Zola's, *La Canaille* spread through the cigar factory like wildfire. The workers

picked which novel the *lector* would read next. The men wanted Zola's novel, but the women were against it.

"Sal, this filthy novel contains graphic sexual descriptions that are demeaning to young women," Chucho argued.

"I don't give a shit what the women think; this novel is a bestseller in France and banned in Spain. All my buddies back in Galicia rave about it. I'm voting to have the *lector* read it. How about you, Chucho? Are you with us or against us?" He bundled fifty cigars and placed them on his workbench.

"I'm not against you, Sal, but women workers are already pelted with sexual innuendo and macho come-ons every day. Reading this novel will be like pouring gasoline on a fire." He put away his *chaveta* knife, covered the gluepots, and stashed a couple of cigars in his shirt.

"So, what's it going to be, *amigo*? Yes or no?" Sal stood in Chucho's path leading to the door.

"I haven't decided yet, Sal. Please stand aside." A hot rush filled Chucho's body. He clenched his fists.

"I always knew you Mexicans were a bunch of pussies. I never should have trusted you. I took you into my home and this is what you do to me?" His voice got louder. "In Galicia we take guys like you and cut their balls off." Sal pushed Chucho to the floor, kicked his backside and showered the downed man with punches until he was too winded to hit any more. At that point, Chucho jumped to his feet and kicked Sal in the stomach. Sal crumpled to the floor, out of breath, vulnerable. Chucho did not hit him again; he simply walked away.

The next morning Sal showed up at the factory at ten o'clock wearing a black cloak and a Spanish beret called a *boina*. He marched over to their workbench. "Please stand, Senor Sanchez." He tossed a soft leather glove on the table and stabbed it with a nine-inch stiletto.

"Six o'clock, Sunday morning, Rocky Point Beach. Bring a gun." He wheeled on his boot-heels and strode out.

On Saturday night, Lydia went shopping at Penney's department store on Seventh Avenue. A year ago, she and Chucho had had their first kiss in one of the dressing rooms on this floor and had been meeting secretly ever since. He saw her lingering in the lingerie section, a troubled look on her face.

"Thank God you came, Chucho! We don't have much time; I have to fix dinner for Sal. Did you get my message?"

"Yes. No one saw me."

"Chucho, *mi amor*, I'm pregnant. It's your baby. You're the only man I've made love with. Sal hasn't touched me in years." She Cried, he held her. "Please, don't be angry with me."

"Angry? Why should I be angry? This child is a gift from the gods. I'm overjoyed."

"But those same gods could take you away from me tomorrow"

"Have no doubt, *querida*, I will triumph over Sal and marry his widow. I love you Lydia, say you'll marry me."

At sunrise on Sunday, a cold front whips across Tampa Bay and frosts the tips of banana leaves. Strong winds sway palm trees and big waves roll in at Rocky Point Beach. It's six a.m. and the duel is about to begin. Chucho and Sal sit at opposite ends of a long table, awaiting final instructions. In the crowd, wagers are being laid on the outcome of the duel.

"Senor Sanchez, since you have no next of kin, who do you authorize to claim your body and give you a proper burial?" asks the referee.

All Chucho can think of is Lydia and the baby. Sal is already getting suspicious, so there's little to lose. "I name La Senora Lydia Fernandez to claim my body," he broadcasts to the crowd.

"What?" Sal jumps to his feet. "Are you crazy? You want my wife to be your angel?" He bends over, nose to nose with Chucho. "I'll never let her do that, you little heathen. I should blow your head off right now."

"Please, Don Salvador, we must leave new personal conflicts out of this," intones the referee. Then he inspects the guns, lays a long black ribbon on the ground to mark the starting line, and crosses himself. Sal's supporters are all Spanish, mostly *Gallego* businessmen, and a doctor. Only a few Cuban cigar-makers, some of them black, stand on Chucho's side.

"*Estimados* Senores, we are here to settle, once and for all, a dispute between our friends, Don Salvador and Don Jesus. Please stand, Gentlemen."

Sal and Chucho come to their feet and glare at each other.

"In a minute," says the referee, "You will pick up your weapon. Point it at the sky, and keep it there until it's time to line up." He bows his head. "Dear Father in heaven, please forgive us for what we are about to do. God have mercy on our souls. Amen."

The two men stand back to back at the starting line, pistols pointed skyward.

"Wait until you hear the starting shot," says the referee. "I'll count the first step. On the count of ten, you are free to turn around and fire. May the best man win."

The starting gun cracks a shot into the cold winter air, and the referee begins to count: "One . . . two . . . three . . ." The duelists walk in opposite directions, weapons held high. ". . . four . . . five . . . six . . ."

On the count of six, Chucho spins around and shoots Sal's driver, who had cocked a small pistol and aimed at him from the crowd. Sal turns and they both fire away at each other at point-blank range.

A bullet pierces Sal's head and he spirals to the ground in a seizure. Chucho falls flat on his back, arms spread wide and feet crossed, a large bloodstain spreading on his chest like an opening flower. The crowd remains silent as a doctor examines the bodies.

"Both duelists are dead, and so is the driver," Doctor Gavilla pronounces. "Bring the wagon and take them to the morgue."

When Lydia gets the news that both her husband and her lover are dead she is at the factory stripping tobacco leaves. Her head drops to the bench; she wails and curses the gods. Co-workers comfort her. Later that day she goes to the morgue with a friend to claim the bodies of the two men. The coroner meets her at the door.

"Your husband's body will be transferred to the funeral home as you asked, Senora Fernandez. But the Mexican has come back to life. I detected his shallow breathing as we wheeled the corpse into the cooler. We rushed him to the Centro Austuriano Hospital, where the surgeon removed a bullet from his breastbone and revived him. He is in good condition and resting peacefully."

As soon as Sal's death certificate is finalized, a Notary Public marries Lydia and Chucho in his hospital room. A doctor and nurse witness the bedside nuptials.

Soon afterwards, the happy couple moves to Chucho's hometown of Morelia, Mexico, and are re-married in a traditional Mexican Catholic wedding. His uncles and male cousins dress in shiny blue suits, the women wear pink floor-length gowns, and the bride is radiant in a lovely white maternity wedding dress. Chucho, Jr,—ten pounds, olive skin, Aztec features—arrives one month later.

SCHOOL DAZE
(1943-1956)

I remember skipping barefoot on hot sands, tree shade to tree shade, on the first day of school at Orange Grove Elementary.

I remember marching down stone hallways in the boys' line, past arched portals opening into a wide lawn with a flagpole at the center.

I remember plowing sandy soil outside our classroom window to plant a Victory Garden.

I remember performing in a white-sequined outfit for the "Silver and White Ballet" at the May Festival.

I remember riding a train for the first time on a field trip to the Ringling Brothers Circus in Sarasota. A giraffe threw up all over me.

I remember stealing a watermelon from Mr. Ames' farm. My buddies and I plugged the hot moist fruit and took turns humping it.

I remember pedaling five miles to Washington Junior High School on my first bicycle built from spare parts found in junkyards.

I remember joining the marching band in the seventh grade to avoid taking showers with the other boys in P.E class. I played French horn.

I remember writing love poems to Marilyn Monroe in the ninth grade. The teacher confiscated them.

I remember scoring in the top tier of achievement tests, though my grades languished in the cellar. I never took a book home.

I remember dancing every tune with a different girl at teen dances. Most of the other boys couldn't dance.

I remember editing Jefferson High's first "cheesecake" calendar with glossy photos of high-school girls in beach attire and cheerleader uniforms. I wrote a poem for each month.

I remember dating homecoming queens in high school while secretly lusting after the long-legged players on the basketball team.

I remember necking with my high school sweetheart on a date, then making out with an older gay man after midnight in the next town.

I remember delivering mail like Jimmy Olsen to writers in the *Tampa Tribune* newsroom. I dreamed I'd be a reporter someday.

I remember graduating from high school, and only my Aunt Maria sat in the auditorium. The rest of my family went to my brother's wedding in Miami.

I remember enrolling in the fall semester at the University of Tampa, but never going to classes; then dropping out and joining the Navy.

I remember falling in love with my bunkmate in a barracks filled with nude and semi-nude eighteen-year olds. I could no longer deny my feelings for other men.

YBOR DREAMING

I drift down palm-lined avenues
Past backyards ripe with avocadoes
Papayas, and guavas. I savor a cognac
And *café solo* with cigar-makers who roll
The finest Havanas in the world.

I see electric streetcars swoosh down
La Setima to Palmetto Beach and Ballast Point.
I order a pressed sandwich, thin slices of Spanish ham,
Roast pork and cheese on Cuban bread at the Silver Dollar Cafe.

I hear fishermen hawk their catch to
Housewives in shotgun houses with small
Porches where workers sit in the evening
And sing Cuban *boleros* and Argentine tangos.

I awake to the aroma of coffee roasting
At La Naviera, bread baking in Alessi's brick oven
And devil crabs steaming at Miranda's. I hear
The blast of ship's whistles at the Ybor docks
Unloading bananas and sea turtles.

I dance to the Caribbean rhythms of bongos,
Timbales and congas, six trumpets and
A bank of saxophones at the Cuban Club.
Mambos, rhumbas, and cha-chas excite my blood.

I cruise down Seventh Avenue in pressed
Khakis to meet the right girl, treat her to a hot
Cuban sandwich at Cuervo's, a *pastel de pina* at
Las Novedadas, or a mango sherbet at Los Helados.

I see my parents, uncles, and cousins lose their jobs
To cigar-making machines installed after the War.
Families move away, children flee town
And never come back.

I awake to the thunder of bulldozers storming
Across the landscape to make room for an Interstate.
Only brick factories and social clubs remain in
A sea of empty lots dotted with fruit trees.

I mourn those years of neglect, decay, boarded-up
Storefronts, and crime-infested streets.
But Ybor City survives and comes back as a tattooed tart
Luring rowdies to drink and raise hell in dark bars
That serve singles, bikers, gays and blacks.

I watch semi-nude dancers gyrate to disco music
In front of Goya's murals. I see a gay bathhouse on
The same block where I played hopscotch and jump-rope.
A 20-screen multiplex eclipses El Centro Español, where we
Danced to the orchestras of Peréz Prado and Tito Fuentes.

I return to my dream and stand on the corner of
Fifteenth Street and Seventh Avenue and see you
Radiant and alive again.

I hear hot salsa rhythms pouring from
Wrought-iron balconies, trolleys screeching
At the turn and the shuffle of *chaveta* knives
Trimming tender tobacco leaves.

I smell the spicy aroma of Spanish bean soup, and
See waiters carrying two-gallon pots of steaming coffee
To the cigar-makers in the galleries, where *lector*s stand
On platforms and read Cervantes and Tolstoy to the workers.

Ybor of my dreams, I miss you.